I didn't see the ball coming until it was too late.

"Watch out!" I heard. Then a ball hit me square in the shoulder. It threw me off balance, and I fell down. Before I could get up, Pete Millrose was standing over me.

"Are you all right?" Pete asked.

I scrambled to my feet. "Fine," I said, brushing myself off. I rubbed my shoulder.

"Sorry," Pete said. "The ball went out of control." His sandy brown hair blew in the wind. He gave me a big grin, and I could feel myself turning into mush. "You're sure you're okay?"

I looked into Pete's sparkling blue eyes. He was so good–looking that for a moment I couldn't speak. "Fine," I finally said, my voice squeaking. "You can bump into me any time."

"I'll do that," Pete said. Turning suddenly, he ran off to rejoin his friends.

"Gosh," squealed Annie. "I can't believe you said that."

"You know," I said, "Pete's one of the most popular boys in the class. If he and I become friends, I'll bet all the In Crowd girls will want to become friends with me, too."

"Shh," Annie said, grabbing my arm.

"Kathy," a voice said sharply. I turned around. There, with an angry expression on her perfect face, stood Zan Rocksberry, the most popular girl in the sixth grade.

What's New in Sixth Grade?

Mindy Schanback

Cover by Susan Tang

Troll Associates

Library of Congress Cataloging-in-Publication Data

Schanback, Mindy.
    What's new in sixth grade? / by Mindy Schanback.
        p.   cm.—(Making the grade)
    Summary: Kathy endangers her budding friendship with the new girl
next door by ignoring her in favor of the In Crowd at school.
    ISBN 0-8167-2388-5 (lib. bdg.)   ISBN 0-8167-2389-3 (pbk.)
    [1. Friendship—Fiction.   2. Popularity—Fiction.   3. Schools—
Fiction.]   I. Title.   II. Series: Making the grade (Mahwah, N.J.)
PZ7.S33375Wh   1992
[Fic]—dc20   90-26792

A TROLL BOOK, published by Troll Associates

Printed in the United States of America.

10   9   8   7   6   5   4   3   2

What's New in Sixth Grade?

◆

To my parents.
They are always "in" with me.

◆ *Chapter 1* ◆

I divide the girls in my sixth-grade class into the hair spray people and the non-hair spray people. The hair spray people wear eye shadow and talk about boys. They also wear bras.

The thing about the hair spray people is that they don't speak to anyone but each other. It's pretty rude when you think about it. But what's amazing is that everyone wants to be friends with them anyway. Why? Because they're the In Crowd, that's why.

I'm not exactly sure why some people are in and other people are out. Sometimes I think it's just that they decided they were in, and no one had the guts to argue with them.

But, lucky for me, I don't have to worry about all that In Crowd, Out Crowd stuff. I have a best friend, and we don't need anyone but each other. Still, every now and again, I wonder what it would be like to be in the In Crowd. And I know Annie—she's my best friend—does, too.

I was standing in my closet thinking about this one morning when the door to my room banged open.

"Sorry," Annie yelled, running into my bedroom. Annie is little and skinny, and she's got a big head of curly red hair. I think her hair is pretty, but she hates it. She's always trying some new way to straighten it, like putting it on top of her head and wrapping it around a big coffee can. Once she burned a whole hunk of it off trying to iron it.

"Kathy Hayes," she said sternly, "do you know what day it is?"

"September 21st?"

"Today is election day, the day you are running for class president, and you're still not dressed."

I looked down at my underwear. "I know. I can't decide what to wear." I pointed to the floor of my closet. It was covered with various outfits I had tried on and discarded.

"Oh, Kathy. You're hopeless," Annie said as she began rummaging through my closet.

We heard my mother's voice. "If you don't get moving, you'll be late for school."

"Okay," I yelled.

Annie handed me a pair of tight black pants and a baggy pink sweater. I began putting them on.

"There's another reason you can't move away," I said. "If you don't pick out my clothing for me, I'll end up going to school in my underwear."

"I'm sure my dad will find that a real convincing argument," Annie said. Annie's dad got a new job in another town about two hours away. Since then, he's been trying to sell their house so he can have a shorter commute. Their house has been for sale for so long, I don't think they'll ever really move. At least I hope they won't.

I finished dressing, then spun around in front of the mirror. "What do you think?" I asked.

"Fabulous," she said. "Not only will you

be elected class president in that outfit, but when Pete sees you, he'll faint."

I giggled.

Pete Millrose is the cutest guy in the entire sixth grade. And he's the nicest, too. I knew this to be a fact, even though I'd only gotten up the nerve to talk to him twice. Once I accidentally bumped into him in the hallway. He didn't notice, but I said "excuse me" anyway. The second time was better. I asked him if I could borrow a pencil, and he said he didn't have one. Not the stuff of great romance, but just thinking about it made my skin tingle.

"You're thinking about Pete again," Annie said.

"How can you tell?" I asked.

"It's that goofy look you get," Annie said, giggling.

"Girls. I mean it. Now!" Mom called in her no-nonsense voice. Most of the time, Mom is really nice, but she's a maniac when it comes to eating breakfast. And by breakfast Mom doesn't mean grabbing a bagel on the run. She means a sit-down meal of juice, pancakes, French toast, or eggs.

"Coming," I yelled.

I grabbed my books and ran downstairs.

Annie, her red hair already coming out of her barrettes, was right behind me.

Dad and my little brother Andrew were just leaving as Annie and I sat down at the table. A few seconds later, Mom bustled in carrying a large plate of French toast. "My, don't you look lovely," Mom said to me.

Like I said, Mom is really nice. And she's pretty for a mom, too. Unfortunately, I take after my dad. It's not that I'm bad looking or anything. I have long, wavy, brown hair, and nice, even features. Even so, if I had my choice, I'd want to be the three B's—beautiful, blond, and busty.

It was already late, so I gobbled down my French toast. I kissed Mom good-bye, and Annie and I ran out the door.

"Guess what?" I said to Annie as we walked to school.

"What?"

"Yesterday, Zan Rocksberry actually spoke to me."

"No," Annie said in amazement. "Really?"

"Yeah," I said. "She said, 'That Delia really smells, doesn't she?'"

"Wow," Annie said. "What did you say?"

"I said, 'Yeah, she sure does.'"

Zan is the leader of the hair spray people,

and the prettiest girl in the entire sixth grade. She's the three B's all over, and she knows it, too.

"Does she?" Annie asked.

"Does she what?" I said.

"Does she smell?"

"Who?"

"Who are we talking about? Delia."

"I don't know, Annie," I said in an exasperated voice. "I never smelled her."

"I'll have to sniff her out," Annie said. She looked thoughtful. "Why do you think Zan started speaking to you?"

"I think it's my good looks and charming personality," I said.

Annie cracked up.

"Hey," I said, punching her lightly on the arm, "it's not that funny."

A few minutes later, Annie and I rounded the corner to the school yard. Delia Judd came running up behind us. Unlike all the other girls, who were dressed in tight pants and big tops, Delia was wearing a dress that looked like it was two sizes too big. She also wore thick tights. I knew Delia's family didn't have much money. She was probably wearing her sister's hand-me-downs. Poor, smelly, unfashionable Delia, I thought.

"I saw the shadow of a vampire last night," Delia confided. I had no idea what to say to that, so I just stood there. Behind Delia I could see Annie sniffing, trying to see if Delia smelled.

"Annie, cut it out!" I yelled. Delia turned around, confused, then ran over to the jungle gym.

"What a dork," Annie said nodding her head toward Delia.

"I know," I said. "Still, how would you like it if someone was going around sniffing you?"

"She didn't know," Annie said.

At that moment, Zan walked onto the playground. On either side of her were her two best friends, Rochelle and Lauren.

The In Crowd girls went to the corner of the playground and took out their hair spray and mirrors. First they bent their heads down and brushed their hair forward. After that, they began spraying. They sprayed until their hair looked like shellacked wood. They stood bent over as their hair spray dried in the sun. Then they bent their heads back into a normal position and brushed their hair from the top, styling it back into shape. Then they sprayed that, too.

"I bet you could bounce bricks off their heads," Annie whispered.

I was so busy watching Zan that I didn't see the ball coming until it was too late. "Watch out!" I heard. Then a ball hit me square in the shoulder. It threw me off balance, and I fell down. Before I could get up, Pete Millrose was standing over me.

"Are you all right?" Pete asked.

I scrambled to my feet. "Fine," I said, brushing myself off. I rubbed my shoulder.

"Sorry," Pete said. "The ball went out of control." His sandy brown hair blew in the wind. He gave me a big grin, and I could feel myself turning into mush. "You sure you're okay?"

I looked into Pete's sparkling blue eyes. He was so good-looking that for a moment I couldn't speak. "Fine," I finally said, my voice squeaking. "You can bump into me any time."

"I'll do that," Pete said. Turning suddenly, he ran off to rejoin his friends.

"Gosh," squealed Annie. "I can't believe you said that."

"I know. I'm so embarrassed, I could die."

"No," said Annie, shaking her head, "you were great."

"You really think so?" I asked.

"Really."

"You know," I said, "Pete's one of the most popular boys in the class. If he and I become friends, I'll bet all the In Crowd girls will want to become friends with me, too."

"Shh," Annie said, grabbing my arm.

"Kathy," a voice said sharply. I turned around. There, with an angry expression on her perfect face, stood Zan Rocksberry.

♦ Chapter 2 ♦

"*H*i, Zan," I said brightly. Zan nodded. Of course Rochelle and Lauren were by her side. Rochelle and Lauren nodded, too. They probably can't move by themselves, I thought. Still, having three people stare at me was making me jittery.

Then I remembered my dad saying that people loosen up when you compliment them. "It's great the way you put on that hair spray," I said.

"Thank you," Zan said.

"Really great," I continued, encouraged. Zan was silent.

"Boy, that Delia really smells, doesn't she?" I said nervously.

"I hear you're running for class president," Zan said, tossing her long white-blond hair.

"Running for class president," said Lauren.

I tried to strike a casual pose by leaning back against the school wall. But the wall wasn't where I thought, and I almost fell down.

"That's right," I said, my voice squeaking. Then in my coolest voice, "What do you think?"

"I'm going to run, too," Zan said.

"Run, too," said Lauren.

I let out a groan. "Oh no. If you run, I'll never win."

"That's right," Zan said sweetly. "So maybe you shouldn't run. Then it will be unanimous."

"Shouldn't run," Lauren said. What was this girl, a parrot?

Before I could think of anything else to say, the bell rang. We turned and went to line up at the door. "Can you believe she's running?" Annie asked.

I shook my head. "Well, I might as well not run."

"Oh no you don't, Kathy," said Annie. "You're running because I'm nominating you, and that's final."

I looked down at the ground. "But I won't win," I whispered.

"Maybe, maybe not," Annie said. "But you definitely won't win if you don't run." I nodded. I knew Annie was right. The second bell rang and we filed into school.

"Okay, class," our teacher, Mrs. Kampton, said after we settled into our seats. "Today we vote for class president. As you know, the class president is the leader of the class. If I have to be out of the room for any reason, the class president will take over." She took a deep breath. "Any nominations?"

Annie stood up. "I nominate Kathy Hayes," she said loudly. Zan turned around in her chair and gave her a mean look.

Mrs. Kampton smoothed down her short, jet-black hair. Then she carefully wrote "Kathy Hayes" on the blackboard.

Rochelle Baker stood up. She's probably the richest girl in the class. "I nominate Zan Rocksberry," she said.

"And I second it," said Lauren, standing up.

"Any other nominations?" Mrs. Kampton said. She looked around the room.

Zan raised her hand. "No one seconded Kathy Hayes' nomination," she said.

"I don't think that will be necessary," Mrs. Kampton said.

"*Robert's Rules of Order* says that all nominations should be seconded," argued Zan.

"I second it," Delia yelled. I looked at Delia gratefully. She might be a dork, but at least she was a dork for Kathy Hayes.

"There you go," Mrs. Kampton said to Zan. "Nominated and seconded. Okay, class, we'll vote by secret ballot. Everyone take a piece of paper and write down who you're voting for. I'll count the votes while you work on some math problems."

I tore a piece of paper out of my notebook and wrote my own name in capital letters. Like everyone else in the class, I folded my ballot into quarters. Then I passed it up to the front of the room.

Mrs. Kampton unfolded the papers, and put them into two neat piles. I sneaked a look. They looked pretty even. Maybe I did better than I thought.

Mrs. Kampton counted the piles. "The vote was very close," she said. "But we do have a winner." I could feel the muscles in my body tightening.

"Zan Rocksberry." Zan stood up and the class applauded.

I applauded, too, real hard. I had this big, phony smile pasted on my face, like I was just thrilled with the results. It was horrible.

The morning seemed to drag on forever. Finally it was over. After lunch, Annie and I sat outside on the steps. I was surprised at how many people came over and said they voted for me.

Finally, we were alone. "Oh well," I said.

"Next year," said Annie.

I looked across the playground to where Zan and her group were busy applying eye shadow. "Not likely," I said glumly. The bell rang.

Zan and her friends walked over and stood on line behind us. "Good try," Zan said. "You did very well considering you were running against me."

"Thanks," I said. I was smiling at her like

an idiot. What is it about Zan that makes me act so weird, I wondered.

Our first class after lunch was gym. I happen to hate gym. It's not that I'm a bad athlete. It's just that I can never understand what everyone gets so worked up about when they play sports. Annie, who loves sports, says I have no killer instinct.

The other thing I hate about gym is that you have to change in front of everybody. I don't mind changing in front of Annie, but changing in front of everyone gives me the creeps. I usually sneak off and change in the bathroom.

But today, the janitor was doing repairs in the bathroom, so it was closed off. I had to change next to my locker. I pulled off my shirt and put on my little yellow gym suit. Then I noticed it. Almost all of the girls were wearing bras.

I buttoned up my gym suit as fast as I could, and ran over to Annie. "Annie," I whispered. "Practically everyone but us is wearing a bra."

"I know," Annie said glumly.

I could hear Zan giggling and whispering to Rochelle. "Such a baby," she said. I was

sure she was talking about my braless con-
dition.

I was determined that whether I needed
one or not, I was going to get a bra today.

◆ Chapter 3 ◆

*T*he afternoon seemed to go on forever. All I could think about was how to convince Mom I needed a bra. But I knew no matter how I started, I'd end up saying, "Come on, Mom. Everyone wears one."

Then she'd say, "If everyone jumped off a cliff, would you?" Mom always says that.

Suddenly the classroom was very quiet. "Kathy." I looked around. "Kathy," Mrs. Kampton said again.

"I'm sorry, Mrs. Kampton," I said. "I wasn't paying attention."

"Well, do," Mrs. Kampton said sternly. "It

would help if you opened your book to page twenty-four like everyone else."

I was so lost in my own thoughts that I had no idea what we were studying. I glanced around to see what text we were using.

"Your science book," Mrs. Kampton said in an annoyed voice. The class giggled.

"I'm sorry, Mrs. Kampton," I said again. I fumbled around for my book. When I looked up, I saw Pete smiling at me. I smiled back.

"Kathy!" Mrs. Kampton yelled. I opened my science book and found page twenty-four. I tried hard to pay attention, but my mind kept drifting.

Finally the day was over. I made it home in about three seconds flat.

I told Mom about the election. "I'll never win Mom, not against the In Crowd."

"What's important is that you did your best," Mom said. "And you know, these things have a way of changing. The person who's in one day can easily be out the next."

My mom tried hard, but she didn't know Zan. I decided to change the subject. "Mom, I need a bra." So much for leading up to it gradually.

"Well, let's get you one right now," Mom said. "I have to go to the store and buy your brother a pair of jeans anyway."

"That's it?" I yelped. "You're not going to say that I'm too young or that it's a stupid idea?"

"I was young and silly once myself," Mom said, smiling.

"Very funny," I muttered, but secretly I was pleased. Mom thought I was old enough for a bra!

Mom, Andrew, and I went downtown to Luger's Department Store. Andrew is seven. He's quiet and shy and everyone says he's a genius. In fact, he is so smart that he skipped second grade. I know that's supposed to be great, but I feel bad for him. Now he's in third grade with a bunch of kids he doesn't even know.

We bought Andrew some jeans, then the three of us walked into the teen department. I made a beeline to the underwear counter.

Andrew and Mom followed. "Mom," I whispered.

"Yes," she whispered back.

"Andrew," I said, pointing at him.

"Andrew?" Mom said.

"Mom!" Sometimes my mother just doesn't get it.

Suddenly, it was like a light clicked on in her head. "Ah!" Mom said. She rummaged around in her purse, then handed Andrew a bunch of quarters. "Here, Andrew," she said. "Why don't you go play some video games on the main floor? We'll meet you there when we're done."

Andrew took the coins and ran off toward the escalators.

"Come on, Mom," I said, grabbing her arm. I pulled her over to the bra counter.

"Can I help you?" a saleslady asked.

Mom looked at me, but I was too embarrassed to speak. "We'd like to look at some bras for the young lady," Mom said.

"What size are you?" the saleslady asked me.

"Small," I said.

"I meant your back," the saleslady said.

"Oh," I said. I blushed a deep shade of red.

"First time?" the saleslady said, smiling.

I nodded. She looked at me, her eyes narrowing slightly. "You're about a size thirty," she said.

"Thirty what?" I asked.

"Thirty training bra," she said.

I looked down at my flat chest and sighed.

"These should fit you," the saleslady continued, pointing to a rack of bras behind me.

Mom and I looked through the bras. I touched a black lacy one. "This one is nice," I said.

Mom shuddered. She picked through the rack until she found four models she liked. They were all white or beige and very simple. Together we went into the dressing room.

I began trying on bras. "Hello," the saleslady sang, sticking her head through the curtains. "How are we doing?" I crouched in the corner. Didn't anyone ever teach her to knock?

"We're doing fine," Mom said with a feeble smile. The saleslady disappeared.

I wanted the black lace bra. Mom wanted me to get one of the stretchy ones. In the end we compromised. Two white stretchies and a black lacy. I decided to wear the black lacy one home.

As soon as we pulled into the driveway, I

dashed to Annie's house. The door was open and I rushed in. "Annie," I yelled. "I got three bras."

I skidded into the kitchen. "And that's the refrigerator," Annie was saying to three strangers. "You can see it's very old."

"Hi, Annie," I said weakly.

"Hi, Kathy," she said. "These are the Krimleys. They're interested in buying the house."

I shook hands with Mr. and Mrs. Krimley. Then I smiled at the girl, who I thought was about my age. She was tall and skinny with straight brown hair and freckles.

"Hi," the girl said. "My name is Beth. I'm eleven years old and plan to be a great artist."

I was surprised. I was eleven years old, too, and didn't have a clue about what I wanted to be.

Annie continued into the bathroom. "This is the second bathroom." She flushed the toilet. "You have to jiggle it to get it to stop running. Did I mention the plumbing was bad?"

"Yes, you did," Mrs. Krimley replied.

"Good," said Annie. "The roof needs

repairing also." A few minutes later we ushered the Krimleys out of the house.

"Thanks for the tour," Mrs. Krimley said. "It was very enlightening." Then the three Krimleys got into their car.

As soon as they left we broke out laughing. "Did you see their faces when I told them the roof leaked?" Annie said. "It was too funny for words."

"Annie, how could you?" I said.

"Hey," Annie said, "I don't want to move. Do *you* want me to move?"

"You know I don't," I said, hugging her. "How come your mother isn't here?" I asked. "She usually shows the house."

"She had an emergency at work and couldn't make it back in time," Annie said. "So I told her that I'd do it."

"If she knew what you were going to say, she would have rushed right home." We giggled.

We went into the kitchen for some cookies. I showed Annie my new bra. "How do you like it?" I asked.

"Wow!" Annie said. "The In Crowd will die of envy. I bet none of them has a black bra."

About ten minutes later, Annie's mother came home. "I don't know what you did," she told Annie, "but whatever it was, thank you."

"For what?" Annie asked.

Annie's mother smiled. "You just sold the house."

"Sold the house!" Annie screeched.

"That's right," Annie's mother said, kissing her. Then she looked up. "I wonder how they knew the roof leaked?"

◆ Chapter 4 ◆

I couldn't believe it. Annie was really moving. The day after Halloween, our class had a good-bye party for her. All the kids signed a giant card, and we had soda and cake.

All through the party, different kids came over to tell Annie how much they were going to miss her.

"I've never been so popular," Annie whispered to me. "Too bad I can't stick around and enjoy it."

I wanted to laugh, but I felt too sad. Sure, some of the kids were going to miss her a little, but she was my best friend. I was going to miss her a lot.

That afternoon, I went over to Annie's house for the last time. Together we packed up the rest of her stuff. We sat in her room glumly. Neither of us could think of anything to say.

Her mother came in. "Well, if it isn't the gloom and doom twins," she said. She gave us five dollars and sent us to the Sweet Shop. We sat there quietly sucking on ice cream sodas until it was time to leave.

The next morning the moving van came and took all of Annie's stuff away. I watched it until I had to go to school.

School was horrible without Annie. There was nobody to share secrets with. No one knew I was wearing a black lace bra, and I didn't feel like telling anyone either.

I had lunch with Edith Applewhite, Mary Mahony, and Flora Chu. And let me tell you, three duller girls never existed. They're nice, but it was a struggle staying awake when I was with them.

All through lunch, Edith talked about her toenail. Apparently it's ingrown, whatever that means. I mean, who talks about toenails at lunch? It's disgusting.

In science, we were learning the table of elements. Instead of paying attention, I looked around the room, deciding who to be friends with. I rejected one set of girls after another. Either they were too boring, total dorks, or they had best friends already. That left Mary and her friends, or the In Crowd.

So that's it, I thought. I would have to get into the In Crowd or die of boredom. After school, I went out and bought hair spray and eye shadow.

That afternoon I spent a lot of time in the bathroom. I came down to dinner with my new look. Dad and Andrew were reading in the living room. Dad took one look at me and started screaming for my mother. "Margaret. Margaret."

"Do you think it makes me look mature?" I asked, spinning around.

Dad started to sputter. "Mature? Too mature. In my day, girls didn't wear makeup until they were in college. Margaret!"

My mother came into the living room, wiping her hands on her apron.

"Look at Kathy," Andrew said.

Mom looked at me and started to laugh. Then Dad and Andrew started laughing, too.

"This is not funny," I yelled. Then I

turned and marched into my bedroom. Families were so stupid sometimes.

All through November, I ate with Mary, Flora, and Edith. They were dull, but at least they were friendly.

That's more than you could say for Zan and her crowd. I kept trying to make friends with them, but I didn't want to be too obvious. I've seen how mean the In Crowd girls could be when they didn't want you to be in their group.

So, even though I kept trying to make friends with the In Crowd, I took it slow. Every couple of days I'd try something new. I would smile or compliment them. If one of them said something to me, I tried to show an interest. But nothing seemed to work. After a month, they were no friendlier than before.

By the time Thanksgiving rolled around I was ready to give up. Annie and I spoke on the phone every weekend, but I was still pretty lonely.

The first week in December, I saw a van pull up next to Annie's old house. A tall, skinny girl got out. Beth and her family were moving in.

As soon as my mother saw the van, she got busy. In no time flat, she whipped up a casserole of meat and vegetables all covered with mashed potatoes. Shepherd's pie, she called it.

Together we crossed the lawn and knocked on the Krimleys' door. Mrs. Krimley was thrilled to see us. She oohed and ahhed over the shepherd's pie for about an hour. I went to find Beth. She was in Annie's old room.

Beth was holding a paintbrush and staring at the wall in front of her. I was surprised to see that she was painting a big mural on the wall. It looked like a pair of eyebrows with a big eye above and between them.

"Hi Beth," I said.

"I'm painting the third eye," Beth said.

"What's the third eye?" I asked.

"The third eye is located right in the middle of your forehead," said Beth. "It's from the days when people had three eyes. Eventually the third eye disappeared, but it's still the center of consciousness and awareness."

"Where?" I said, touching my forehead.

"Right here," Beth said. She put her finger in the center of my forehead, about half an inch above my eyebrows. "Can you feel it when I press down?"

I couldn't, but I nodded politely. I stood back and looked at what she had drawn. I had to admit that the eye looked pretty lifelike.

"Sure looks like a big eye," I said.

"Thank you. I'm going to cover every inch of these walls with my paintings," said Beth. "Someday people will come and take this room apart piece by piece to preserve my art."

I didn't know if she was right, but I admired her confidence. Mrs. Krimley and my mom came into Beth's room. "This is Beth," Mrs. Krimley said.

"Also known as 'that rotten kid,' " Beth said.

Mrs. Krimley tried to smile. "Beth has a real sense of humor," she said.

"That must be very nice for you," Mom said.

Mrs. Krimley rolled her eyes.

"How old are you, Beth?" my mother asked.

"I'm eleven years old and I'm going to

be a great artist someday," said Beth. Mom looked at the eye she was painting and smiled.

"I see," Mom said. "So, you'll probably be in the sixth grade with Kathy."

"That's right," Beth said. "I registered this morning."

"Who's your teacher?" I asked.

Beth looked at her mother.

"Mrs. Kampton," said Mrs. Krimley.

"You're in Kathy's class," Mom said. "Mrs. Kampton is a very good teacher, isn't she, Kathy?"

"She's okay," I said, nodding.

"Since you're in Kathy's class," Mom continued, "how about if Kathy walks you to school tomorrow?"

"That would be very nice," said Mrs. Krimley.

I was stuck. "Okay. I'll meet you out front around 8:30," I said to Beth.

I was not thrilled. On the way home I yelled at Mom. "What if she's a nerd and I'm stuck walking to school with her every day?" I said.

"Be nice, Kathy. She's new and she needs a friend."

"All right," I said, making a face.

Mom put her arm around me. "That's my girl."

When we got home, Mom asked me to stop by the bowling alley to pick up Andrew.

"Oh, Mom."

"Come on, honey. I would go myself, but it's Andrew's first day of bowling."

"So?" I said.

"So I think he'd feel more comfortable and grown-up if you picked him up," Mom said.

"Okay," I sighed. "How did you get Andrew to go bowling anyway?" I was genuinely curious, because Andrew never showed the slightest interest in sports before. Once Dad took him to a baseball game, and he read all the way through it.

"It was easy," Mom said. "He wanted to go."

"Andrew?" I screeched.

"He said that he wants to make some new friends, and bowling seemed like the easiest sport," Mom said.

"The poor kid must be desperate."

"It's been hard for him, skipping a grade," Mom said. "All of his friends are behind him at school."

"At least they're still in the same school," I said, thinking of Annie.

I strolled over to Saunder's Bowling Alley off of Main Street. Andrew was inside, talking to another little boy.

"Hi, Andrew," I said cheerfully. "How's my favorite bowler?"

"Hi, Kathy," Andrew said. A piece of dark hair fell into his eyes. I went to brush it off his forehead, but he pushed my hand away.

"Cut it out," he said.

"Hello," I said to the little blond boy standing next to him.

The kid looked up at me with the brightest blue eyes I'd ever seen. "Hi," he said shyly.

"This is my friend, Willie," Andrew said, pointing to the boy. "We're going to walk to school together tomorrow."

"Nice to meet you, Willie," I said.

"Kathy, is that you?" I turned around and looked right into the eyes of Pete Millrose. My heart started thumping so fast I could barely speak.

"Hi, Pete. What are you doing here?" I managed to get out.

"I'm picking up my little brother, Willie," he said, ruffling the blond boy's hair.

For once I was glad I had a brother. "That's funny," I said, putting my hand on Andrew's head, "I'm picking up *my* little brother, Andrew."

Andrew pushed my hand off his head. "Get it off," he shouted. I tried to glare at Andrew and smile at Pete at the same time.

"You okay?" Pete asked. "Your face is all scrunched up."

When Andrew and I left the bowling alley a few minutes later, Pete and Willie were waiting. The four of us walked home together. At first, I was so nervous I could barely speak. But it turned out that Pete and I had a lot in common. We were both the oldest of two. We loved English, hot sunny days, and ice cream, and we both hated math and asparagus.

We had just gotten to State Street when who should we run into but Zan Rocksberry. She was wearing tight black pants, a designer parka, and earmuffs.

I looked down at my scraggly jeans and blue wool jacket and sighed. If only I had her clothes. Stop kidding yourself, Kathy, I thought. Even in the greatest designer clothing ever invented, you'll still never look like Zan.

Zan practically knocked Andrew over to get close to Pete. "Hi, Pete. Hi, Kathy," she gushed. We chatted for a minute. Then Pete said, "See ya," and we left her standing there. It was great.

When I got home, I surprised my mother by offering to pick up Andrew every week.

Chapter 5

*T*he next morning, at exactly 8:30 A.M., Beth rang my doorbell. I was still eating breakfast.

"Want some toast?" I said indistinctly.

"You were supposed to meet me at 8:30," she informed me. "My dad says that punctuality is the key to life."

My dad looked up from his newspaper and smiled. "I'll have to meet this man," he said.

"Dad, this is Beth Krimley," I said. "She moved into Annie's old house."

"Nice to meet you," he said, holding out his hand.

"And I'm Andrew," my brother said. "Do you have a little brother?"

"No," said Beth. "I'm an only child." Andrew looked disappointed. He went back to his book.

"Hungry?" I asked.

"Starved," Beth said. She grabbed a piece of toast and started munching on it.

"Did you have breakfast?" Mom asked.

"I had some cereal," Beth replied. "We don't bother with a hot breakfast, because my mom has to get to work early."

Mom got a gleam in her eyes. She went into the kitchen and came back with a plate of hot pancakes.

"Here," she said, putting the plate in front of Beth. "You can always come here and have . . ."

"Mom," I said sharply. I didn't want Mom inviting Beth for breakfast every day. I wasn't even sure if I liked her yet.

When we got outside I took a closer look at her. "You're wearing a dress," I said in an accusing tone.

"No kidding, Sherlock," she replied.

"For your information," I told her, "dresses aren't cool this year."

"I'm an artist," Beth replied. "Cool has

no meaning for me. Besides, my mother wanted me to make a good impression on the teacher."

While we walked to school, I told her about Zan and the rest of the In Crowd.

"They sound awful," Beth said. "What do you want to be friends with them for?"

"Because they're cool, that's why," I said hotly.

"Cool, smool," Beth said. We walked the rest of the way in silence.

The first person we saw when we got to the school yard was Delia. She came right over and introduced herself to Beth.

"Hi, you must be the new girl."

"That's right," Beth said, smiling.

"I think I saw a witch last night," Delia said. Count on Delia to say something really stupid, I thought.

"No kidding," Beth said. "I'm really interested in witches." This I could not believe.

"Oh yeah?" Delia said. "How do you feel about goblins?"

In a minute the two of them were having a spirited conversation about demons. It was actually pretty interesting. More interesting than ingrown toenails, anyway. I was so absorbed in the conversation that I didn't even notice Zan.

"Hi, Kathy," said Zan. She looked Beth up and down. "Who's your little friend?"

"Hi, Zan," I said. "This is Beth. She's new."

"Actually," Beth said, "I'm fairly tall for my age, and I don't like to be referred to as 'your little friend.' "

Delia's mouth dropped open. Zan's eyes got wide and round. "I'll forgive you this time," Zan said to Beth, "but I'd watch it if I were you."

"Thanks for the advice," Beth said politely. The first bell rang and we walked over to the school door to line up.

"Wow," Delia whispered to me. "She's tough."

"You should dump these people," Zan said to me in a loud voice. I looked at Delia and Beth, but both of them were staring straight ahead like they hadn't heard anything.

I didn't say anything either. Then Zan abruptly changed the subject. "I didn't know you and Pete were friends."

Aha, I thought. That's why she's talking

to me. "We're like this," I said, holding up two fingers stuck together.

"Really tight, huh?" she said.

"The tightest," I replied confidently.

The second bell rang and we all trooped into the building. "I think he's really nice. What do you think?" I said to Zan.

"I like him, too," she said.

"Like *like*, or just like?" I asked as we walked into the classroom.

I was patting myself on the back for being so cool, when I tripped over my shoelace. I went flying into my desk and fell down. What a jerk, I thought. I looked up.

"Hi, Kathy," Pete said. He held his hand out. His perfect blue eyes sparkled. For a few seconds I couldn't move. Then I grabbed his hand, and he pulled me up.

"I looked for you on the way to school this morning," Pete said.

"Oh yeah," I said, smiling. "I'm sorry I missed you." I stole a look at Zan. I was scoring points by the thousands.

Mrs. Kampton began class by welcoming Beth to Southside. She made us go around the room and introduce ourselves to Beth. Almost everyone said a little something about themselves. Pete told her that he liked baseball. Mary said she hated math.

Zan was the last person to speak. She gave Beth a chilly look and said, "I'm Zan Rocksberry." Then she sat back down.

We were in the middle of doing a combination science/English project. We had to pick a famous scientist and read his or her biography. Then we had to pretend that our scientist was applying for a job, and write him or her a resume and a letter of recommendation.

I was writing about Madame Curie. "I would highly recommend Madame Curie for the job of radiation specialist," I wrote. "Her contributions to the field have been first-rate. In fact, there wasn't even a field before she began her experiments." I looked up to see Mrs. Kampton standing over me.

"You're almost done with your report, aren't you, Kathy?" Mrs. Kampton asked.

"Yes, Mrs. Kampton."

"Good. Why don't you take Beth to the library so she can pick a scientist to write about," Mrs. Kampton said.

"Sure," I said. I took Beth down the hall and showed her where the library was. We went over to the biography section. While she looked through the books, I thought about Pete.

As if she was reading my mind, Beth said, "Pete likes you."

"He does?"

"Definitely," Beth said. "I can tell about these things."

After a few minutes, Beth picked out a book. "I'm going to do Samuel Morse," Beth said finally.

I scratched my head. I knew that name. "Oh yeah, inventor of the telegram," I said.

"Telegraph," Beth said. "But what nobody knows is that he was also a painter. I'll do my report on that."

"It's supposed to be on a scientist," I said.

"So," said Beth, shrugging her shoulders, "he was definitely a scientist."

"I don't think Mrs. Kampton wants you to work on the art part."

She closed the book with a bang. "Trust me," Beth said.

Beth checked the book out. "Do you want to come over after school?" she asked, smoothing down her straight brown hair. I looked at her. Even with that stupid dress on, she was okay.

"Yeah," I said. "I would."

At lunch the most amazing thing happened. Zan asked me to eat with her. I grabbed my tray and went over to her table. The In Crowd table.

"That new girl is such a dork, don't you think so?" Zan asked me.

"Such a dork," Lauren said.

"She's okay," I said.

"Look," said Rochelle. "She's eating with Delia."

"Birds of a feather," Zan said.

"Two dorky birds," said Rochelle. Then they all laughed. I felt bad, but I laughed, too.

After lunch we went to the playground. Zan turned to me. "Do you have any hair spray?"

"Not with me," I said.

"You can use mine," Zan said. Together we went to the edge of the playground. We started putting on hair spray. I didn't know exactly what I was doing, so I tried to imitate Zan.

The hair spray was really gross. It was all sticky, and it smelled bad. When I was finished, I took a look in Zan's portable mirror. "What do you think?" I asked.

"Fab," Zan said. "Does this girl look fab or what?"

"Fab," said Lauren.

"Really cool," Rochelle said. "Now let's do our eyes."

I got my eye shadow out and carefully applied it. When I was done, the girls assured me I looked wonderful.

"Wow," Beth said when she saw me.

"Pretty cool, huh?" I said, touching my hair.

"Cool?" Beth said. "You look like a raccoon who put his paw in a light socket."

"Thanks a lot," I said. Obviously this girl did not know cool when she saw it.

At the end of the day Zan approached me. "We're going shopping after school," she said. "Do you want to come?"

"I'd love to," I said, completely forgetting about Beth.

That night I called Annie. I told her all about my day. How I wore hair spray and eye shadow and went shopping with the In Crowd.

"And you know what else?" I said to Annie. "They asked me to meet them tomorrow on the playground. We're going to put on our hair spray and eye shadow before class."

"Wow," said Annie. "Sounds to me like you're in the In Crowd."

Finally. I was In.

Chapter 6

*B*y New Year's, I was so cool that it was incredible. After Christmas vacation, Mary Mahony came up to me in the classroom and said hello. She was wearing a really tacky outfit. I looked at her and just said, *"Ewwww."*

Then, when Flora Chu came over to sit with me at lunch, I said to her, "That seat is taken." She got up and walked away without a word.

At first I felt bad, but Zan told me not to worry about how the worms felt. That's what she called everyone who was not in the In Crowd: the worms. Anyway, that kind of thing stopped happening after a while. I pretty much stopped speaking to anyone who wasn't in the In Crowd, except for Beth.

Beth and I had a weird friendship. We walked to school together, but once we got there we didn't speak.

Beth was mad at me the day after I stood her up. "I waited for you after school, and you walked by without even looking at me," Beth complained.

"I know, Beth. I'm sorry," I replied. "I had been wanting to go out with Zan and her friends for such a long time, I honestly forgot we had plans."

"That's not good enough," Beth said.

"I know," I said. "How about if you come and have breakfast with us tomorrow?"

"Okay," Beth said. "But it's not because I forgive you. It's because your mom is a great cook."

So Beth and I drifted into this funny friendship. And the truth was, I liked her better than Zan. In fact, I liked her almost as much as I liked Annie.

Annie told me I should drop the In Crowd and just be friends with Beth. But I didn't want to do that. I liked being in the

In Crowd. I knew that the other kids envied me. And though I wouldn't admit it to anyone, that was fun.

But I didn't want to drop Beth either. All Zan's crowd ever wanted to talk about was boys and clothes, and it got boring. There was something else, too. I didn't have to be phony with Beth. I could just be myself, and she liked me anyway.

With the In Crowd you always had to act cool. Whether something wonderful or horrible happened, you had to act like you didn't care.

When I got an A+ on my Madame Curie paper, I was very excited. I had worked hard on that paper, and I was glad it paid off. But I didn't dare show it. "Oh yeah," I said to Zan when she asked me. "A+, is that a laugh."

"Yeah, really," Zan agreed.

And you always had to pretend that you didn't study. Mom makes me study every night. And I get pretty good grades, too. I studied for two days for my social studies exam. But when Zan asked me about it, I said, "Yeah. I took a look at the material."

"Me, too," Zan said, sounding really bored.

I think she was telling me the truth, because she got a D.

So I managed to have a double life, being friends with Beth in the morning and Zan at school. Zan and Beth never spoke to each other, so I was never put in an awkward situation.

That worked out fine until the end of February. Then, in gym, something terrible happened. First of all we had this strange substitute teacher, Ms. Crystaline. She was old for a gym teacher—about fifty—and very skinny.

"Today, class," Ms. Crystaline said, "we are going to explore the wonders of the Russian folk dance." The class moaned, but Ms. Crystaline didn't seem to notice.

She put a record on the old school phonograph. "Now watch, children."

A song with a lively beat blasted out of the machine. Suddenly this skinny old woman was waving her arms and dancing wildly to the music.

"I can't believe this," Zan whispered. I would have answered, but my mouth was hanging open too wide to speak.

"And now for the finale," Ms. Crystaline

screamed. She dropped into a squatting position and began thrusting her legs out one at a time, keeping time with the music.

"There's no way I'm doing this," Zan said.

"No way," agreed Lauren.

"Now, class," Ms. Crystaline said, "I'm going to divide you into groups of six."

Zan, Rochelle, Lauren, Delia, and Beth were in my group.

"I can't believe we're stuck with these worms," Zan whispered, pointing to Delia and Beth. I could see Beth's face get red, and I knew that she overheard.

"Okay, girls. Let's begin," Ms. Crystaline said. She showed us the steps and started the music. We all joined hands and began dancing.

Delia was really clumsy. She's always bumping into things, or tripping over her own feet. At first she did okay, but then when we were doing the side step, she fell down, taking everyone in the circle with her.

Beth, Delia, and I started laughing, but Zan and her friends didn't find it funny at all.

"This girl is not *too* clumsy," said Zan in

her snobbiest voice. She stood up and began brushing herself off.

"Not *too* clumsy," said Lauren.

"On your feet, girls," Ms. Crystaline called out. "Accidents happen." We danced for a few minutes. Then Delia fell down again. This time, she only brought down the people on either side of her, Beth and Zan. Delia began giggling nervously.

"Are you the clumsiest person alive, or what?" Zan shouted.

Delia abruptly stopped laughing. "Sorry," she whispered.

Zan frowned. "If you can't manage to dance around in a circle," she said, "maybe you should just stay home."

Delia looked like she might cry.

"Hey," Beth said, getting up and putting her arm around Delia. "It was just an accident. Don't make such a big deal out of it."

By this time the whole class was listening. Beth looked at me, asking me for support with her eyes. I looked away. Beth was on her own.

"You think you're so great," Zan said to Beth, "but you're just a little nothing, you know that?"

Ms. Crystaline broke in. "Class, class. I do not permit fighting." She looked at her watch. "Anyway, the period is almost over. You may all go to your lockers and get dressed."

The class broke up. Zan, Rochelle, and Lauren walked swiftly toward their lockers.

Beth stood there looking at me. I didn't know what to say. Finally she spoke. "Thanks for standing up for me, Kathy. Your show of support was really great."

"I'm sorry, Beth," I said. "I feel terrible."

"I don't judge people by how they feel," Beth said. "I judge them by how they act, and your act stinks." Then she turned and marched into the locker room.

That night I really needed to talk to a friend. I called Annie and told her the whole story. When I was done, she asked me some questions.

"Do you like Beth?"

"Yeah, I really like her."

"Now that you know Zan, do you like her?"

"Of course I like her," I said. "She's the most popular girl in the sixth grade."

"I mean if she wasn't the most popular

girl, but just some nobody, would you like her?"

That one I had to think about. "I'm not sure," I finally said.

"You know, when I was at Southside, I really wanted to be with the In Crowd," said Annie. "But now that I'm in a different school I see how silly it was."

"What makes it silly?" I asked.

"You know, I'm all alone here. I've made some friends, but nobody I really like." She sounded like she might cry. Suddenly I felt really bad. I had been so caught up in my own problems that I hadn't even asked Annie how it was going for her.

"Oh, Annie," was all I could say.

"Anyway," Annie said, "it made me realize how important you are to me. I'd be friends with you in this new place, even if no one else could stand the sight of you.

"You know," Annie continued, her voice cracking a little, "all this stuff about In Crowds and Out Crowds is really silly. It has nothing to do with who you really are. What's in isn't whose crowd you're a part of. What's in is what's inside."

After we hung up, I thought a lot about

what Annie had said. Maybe being part of
the In Crowd wasn't as great as I had imag-
ined it. Still, it was better than being a
worm.

◆ Chapter 7 ◆

*T*he next morning Beth didn't show up for breakfast.

"Where's Beth?" Dad asked. "It's not like her to be late."

Mom took the pancakes that were waiting on Beth's plate and put them in the oven. I looked out our window. It had snowed the night before and everything looked clean and bright.

Mom joined me at the window. "March first, and it's still snowing," she said gloomily.

"Got to go," Andrew yelled, startling me. He jumped out of his chair. "I'm meeting Willie in five minutes."

"That's wonderful, Andrew," Mom said. "Don't forget your snow boots." A few seconds later, I heard the door slam.

"I'm so glad Andrew has finally made a friend," Mom said.

"Come on, Mom," I said. "That's old news already."

Mom sat down across from me, her hands wrapped around a steaming cup of coffee. "I don't think you realize how hard it was for him, skipping a grade and all. He's the youngest kid in his class."

"I know, Mother," I said impatiently. Mom and Dad were always talking about how hard it was for Andrew to adjust. How about me? It wasn't easy losing Annie, but no one seemed to care about that.

"You've always made friends so easily," Mom continued. "It's not that way for everyone."

I started thinking about Beth. Were we still friends? "I think I'll go over to Beth's and see what's keeping her," I said.

"That's a good idea," Dad said, getting up from the table. "Maybe she's sick."

Mom wrapped up some pancakes in tin foil. "Here," she said, handing me the package, "give her these, honey."

I took the pancakes. "A hot breakfast is very important," we said together.

I put on my snow boots and ran across the lawn to Beth's door. I rang the bell and waited, but no Beth. I pressed my ear to the door, but I couldn't hear anything inside.

Disgusted, I tossed the pancakes in the garbage can around the side of the house. Then I started to walk to school. I passed by Pete and another boy in my class, Jake Ross. They were walking slowly, tossing a ball back and forth.

"Hi," I yelled over to them.

"Hi, Kathy," Pete said. "I thought you were sick today."

"How come?"

"Because we just saw Beth go by without you. Don't you usually walk to school together?"

"We must have just missed each other," I said.

On the way to school, I thought about it. Beth had deliberately left without me. Well, I finally decided, if she's not speaking to me, then I'm not speaking to her. Still, I felt bad.

Instead of starting the day with math, like

we usually do, Mrs. Kampton made an announcement.

"Class, the sixth-grade spring assembly is coming up. As you know, each class does some kind of performance. Let's talk about what we want to do. Does anyone have any ideas?"

"How about a Russian folk dance?" Delia suggested. All the girls in the class started laughing.

"And you'll do the lead part of the falling girl, I assume," Zan said nastily.

"Shut up, Zan," Beth said.

"We do not tell each other to shut up in my class," Mrs. Kampton said. She put her hands on her hips. "Beth Krimley, you apologize to Zan this instant."

"I'm sorry, Zan," Beth said stiffly.

"I forgive you," Zan said. Beth glared at her, but didn't say anything.

"Any other ideas?" Mrs. Kampton asked.

"How about we do a play?" said Zan. "We could do *Peter Pan*. Pete could play Peter and I could be Wendy."

"Peter Pan is a dork, and I refuse to play him," Pete said firmly. "Besides," he added as an afterthought, "it's baseball season."

"A play is not a bad idea," Mrs. Kampton said. On the blackboard she wrote "play" in capital letters. "But *Peter Pan* is a two-hour play, and each class only gets an hour."

Suddenly everyone started speaking at once.

"How about a concert?" said Jake. "I could play the trumpet."

"I can burp anytime I want," said Clarence.

"We could do a dance," said Mary Mahony. "I know how to tap."

I raised my hand. "I have a great idea. How about a talent show?" I said. "That way Mary could dance and Jake could play the trumpet. The rest of us could come up with some funny skits."

"That's an excellent idea, Kathy," Mrs. Kampton said. "What does the rest of the class think?"

The class thought it was a great idea.

"It's more complicated than you think, kids," Mrs. Kampton warned. "A talent show needs costumes, sets, and a director."

"How about making people responsible for their own costumes?" I suggested.

"And I'll do the sets," Beth said. "I'd love to do that."

I could see Rochelle and Zan whispering. Rochelle raised her hand. "I nominate Zan Rocksberry as director," she said formally.

In a flash, Lauren was standing. "And I second it," she said.

"Does anyone object?" Mrs. Kampton asked. I looked at Beth, but she didn't say anything.

"Okay," Mrs. Kampton said. "Zan is the director."

"Can I be in a skit also?" asked Zan.

"Sure," Mrs. Kampton said. "I'm glad to see you're so enthusiastic."

"What about me?" Delia asked. "I could never go on stage. I'd be too scared."

"You can help me with the sets," Beth offered.

"You know," Mrs. Kampton said, "every show needs a stage manager. The stage manager sees to it that everyone goes on stage on time with the right props. How about that?"

"Ooh," Delia said, her face lighting up with pleasure. "I'd love to do that."

"Come on," Zan said. "She could never manage it. She can't even get her socks to match." Everyone in the room turned to look at Delia's feet. And, although I hadn't noticed before, they were distinctly different shades of blue.

"Who's the teacher here," Mrs. Kampton asked sharply, "me or you?"

Zan looked at her square in the face. "You are, Mrs. Kampton, but as director, I'm responsible for the show."

"I'll help her," Mrs. Kampton said. "You do trust me, don't you?"

Zan nodded. "Yes, Mrs. Kampton."

Mrs. Kampton turned to the rest of the class. "I'll give you a few minutes to talk among yourselves and see what you want to do."

Instantly the room was buzzing with conversation. Mary Mahony, Edith Applewhite, and Flora Chu were going to do a routine from "Singin' in the Rain." Jake and five other kids decided to do a musical number.

Zan immediately took over. She rounded up me, Lauren, Rochelle, Pete, and his two friends Steve and Charlie to be in her group.

"I have a great idea for a skit," Zan said. "It's called *Liar on Fire*. We did it at camp this summer, so we wouldn't have to write it or anything."

"What's it about?" Pete asked.

"I'm the liar," Zan said, "and every time I lie, someone shouts 'Liar, liar, pants on fire.' Then you all take turns putting out the fire. At the end of the skit, someone, maybe you , Kathy, throws water on me—we'll use confetti instead of real water—and I melt. Isn't that a scream?"

She looked around with a big smile on her face.

"Doesn't do it for me," Pete said.

"I'll tell you what," Zan said. "I'll have copies made of the script, and if you don't like it, we'll think of something else."

That sounded fair, so we all agreed. And when Zan showed us the script the next day, we all had to admit that it was pretty funny.

That night Annie called me. I told her all about the talent show. And she told me that she had finally made a friend, Stella Jenkins.

"She's really nice," Annie said enthusiastically. "And she's funny, too."

"That's great, Annie," I told her. But I had a funny feeling in the pit of my stomach. What if she started liking Stella better than me?

*   *   *

The spring assembly wasn't until the end of May, so our class had plenty of time to get ready. Zan really worked hard to get things organized. She had everyone draw up a list of props, which she gave to Delia. At first, Delia kept getting the props for the different acts mixed up. After Zan yelled at her a few times, Delia labeled everything. Then it didn't happen very often.

Zan didn't like any of Beth's ideas for sets, so she cut some pictures out of magazines and asked her to duplicate them. Beth didn't look happy, but she must have agreed, because I saw her take the pictures and put them in her book bag.

Rehearsals were on Mondays. That worked out great for me, because afterward Pete and I could walk to the bowling alley together to pick up our little brothers.

Pete was great, and the more I got to know him, the better I liked him. I knew he liked me, too, but not in the way I liked him. He was always calling me something unromantic like "buddy" or "pal." I bet no one ever called Zan "buddy."

About a month later, I was packing my stuff after rehearsal when I heard Pete call, "Kathy, ready to go?" I turned, planning to smile right into his eyes. Then I saw his arm. Zan was on it, looking as smug as can be. Sometimes I wanted to smack that girl. She knew I liked Pete, so how could she do this to me?

"Yeah," I said.

"Well, wait for me," Pete said.

"I'd love to see your little brother bowl," Zan purred. "I'll come, too."

"I'd love to see your little brother bowl," I muttered to myself. I noticed she didn't want to see *my* little brother bowl.

When we got to the bowling alley, Andrew came running over to me. "Kathy, Kathy, I bowled a 150. That's the best I ever did." I looked down at Andrew's excited face and gave him a big smile.

"That calls for a celebration," I said. "How about I take you to the Sweet Shop for a soda?"

When we finally got home, the phone was ringing. It was Pete.

"Hi, Kathy," he said.

"Hi, Pete. Long time no see."

"Yeah," Pete said. "I wanted to talk to you on the way to the bowling alley, but I couldn't get away from Zan. Would you like to go out with me on Saturday? We could go to a movie, then maybe stop at the Sweet Shop."

"Thank you, Pete," I said, very cool and collected. "I'd love to." I hung up the phone. Then I started screaming.

Chapter 8

*M*om ran in to see what was going on. "I've got a date!" I screamed, jumping up and down. "An actual date." I called Annie.

"Wow," she said after I told her the news. "That's fabulous. And you're the first girl in sixth grade to have a date."

"Yeah," I said proudly.

"Ooh, Zan is going to be so jealous," Annie said.

"I know," I said. I felt a tightening in my stomach. I knew how Zan was when she got jealous.

The next day, while we were putting on our eye makeup, I told Zan and the other girls. Not like I told Annie, of course. No screaming and giggling.

"Oh yeah, and Pete asked me out. We're going to go to a movie and the Sweet Shop. I hope it won't be a drag."

Zan kept her face totally blank. "Depends on the movie, I guess," she said lightly. But the pencil she was holding in her hand snapped in two.

On Friday, Zan came over to help me decide what to wear. "Really, Kathy," she said, looking through my wardrobe. "You have the most primitive clothing."

"Well, do you see anything?" I asked.

"I'm looking," Zan said, flipping through the clothes on the hangers. "Not even I could do much with these clothes."

"Thanks a lot," I said hotly.

"How about this?" she said, taking out a pair of tight black pants and a loose black and white blouse. "It's a good thing loose blouses are in this year, because you have no bust to speak of."

I looked down at my chest. "They've grown a little," I said.

"You'd have to have a magnifying glass to notice," Zan said. She handed me the clothes she'd picked out.

"I would wear something better," she said, "but this should do for you."

"Thanks," I said sarcastically. "You're a real pal."

"I know," Zan said seriously. "So how are you going to act?"

"I don't know. Like I always do, I guess."

Zan looked at me and shook her head. "Do that and you won't get asked out again. The most important thing on a date is to act hard to get. My sister says that men love the thrill of the chase. Once they know you like them, they lose interest."

"Pete already knows I like him," I said.

Zan shrugged. "Do it your way, then," she said, "but don't say I didn't warn you."

That night I called Annie and asked her opinion. "No, no," she said. "I don't think you should act hard to get at all. My cousin Sue says the most important thing is to show an interest. She says guys love talking about themselves, so you should ask them lots of questions."

"Like what?"

"I don't know. Their shoe size, maybe." She giggled.

"Thanks a lot," I said.

Mom also gave me some advice. "Just be yourself, honey."

How in the world was I going to show an interest, act hard to get, and be myself, all in the same evening?

On Saturday, Pete picked me up promptly at seven. I introduced him to my parents and we stood around talking for a few minutes.

"Take good care of my little girl," Dad said as we were leaving. His little girl? Really!

"Nice night," I said, looking around.

"Yeah. Real springy," Pete replied. He walked very fast with his hands in his pockets. I had to practically run to keep up. Luckily the movie theater was only a couple of blocks away.

Pete bought our tickets. "Popcorn?" he asked.

"Yes, please," I said. We got a big container and sat down.

During the movie, Pete and I ate our popcorn out of the same container. Our fingers kept touching. Then Pete grabbed my hand. His was sticky and buttery, but I held it anyway.

After the movie we walked over to the Sweet Shop. I tried to show an interest. "What does your dad do?"

"He's an electrician."

"Oh, that's interesting. Are you interested in doing that sort of work?"

"Maybe."

"So what about your mom?"

"What about her?"

"What does she do?"

"She's a secretary. What is this, twenty questions?"

"Sorry," I said meekly.

"It's all right," Pete said. "It's me. I just hate it when people ask me a lot of questions." So much for that advice, I thought. Maybe I should try acting hard to get.

Pete held the door to the Sweet Shop open and we walked to a booth in the back. I held myself very tall. I wanted everyone to see that I was on a date. Unfortunately, the only person I knew was Maggie Layton, a twelfth grader who used to baby-sit for me and Andrew. She came over to say hello.

"She's pretty, don't you think?" I asked Pete after she left.

"Too much makeup," Pete said. "All that

hair spray and . . ." Suddenly he stopped talking and his face got red.

"You don't like hair spray and makeup?" I asked.

"Well, I . . ."

"Tell the truth."

"It's okay, I guess," he mumbled. "I mean no, not really."

I could feel my eyes filling with tears.

"You should know this if you're going to be my girlfriend," Pete said seriously.

"Your girlfriend," I said in a little voice. I felt my heart doing flip-flops.

"Yeah," he said, looking down.

"I don't know," I said.

Pete looked up at me. "Well, if you don't want to . . ."

This was no time to act hard to get. "I want to. I want to," I said quickly. Pete looked up and gave me a big smile.

I couldn't believe it. I was Pete's girl-friend!

Chapter 9

*O*n Monday, Pete met me on the corner and we walked to school together. All the kids turned to look at us when we got to the school yard. I was embarrassed, but proud, too.

Pete went over to Jake and his other friends and began playing catch. I joined Zan and her gang. They were putting on hair spray and eye shadow. I refused to put any on.

"You're such a baby," Zan said.

"I'm just trying to please my man," I said. I heard that in a movie once.

"What did Pete say about it?" Rochelle asked.

"He said he liked the natural look," I said.

"I wonder if Jake likes the natural look, too?" Rochelle said. Jake Ross was her current crush.

"I think all guys prefer the natural look," I said firmly.

A few days later Rochelle stopped using hair spray and eye shadow. Then Zan showed up without hair spray and eye shadow. Instead she wore colored shoelaces in her sneakers. Hair spray and eye shadow were out, colored shoelaces were in.

Pete and I went out on another date. Well, we didn't exactly go out. My mom asked me to baby-sit for Andrew one afternoon, so I invited Pete over. He and Andrew played ball. Then we watched TV until my dad came home from work.

While Andrew was upstairs, Pete kissed me. We were watching television when I heard the garage door open.

"My dad is back," I said.

Looking nervous, he leaned over and kissed me quickly on the lips. It happened so fast that I didn't have time to do anything.

I could hear the key turn in the lock. "I'm home," Dad called out in a cheery voice.

Later that night I called Annie. I told her all about my kiss. Then we started talking about school. The year was almost over, and we were both bored. "It seems like we've been studying Russia forever," I said.

"That's how I feel about magnetism," Annie replied. "Stella and I are doing a science project on it."

"You and Stella sure spend a lot of time together," I said. It wasn't that I was jealous or anything. I was glad she had found a friend. "Are you going to be here next weekend?" I asked.

"Yes, my parents said it was okay. I can't wait to see you and the sixth-grade assembly," Annie said. I could tell she meant it.

"I can't wait to see you, too," I said happily.

Dress rehearsal for the assembly was a disaster. Delia kept giving everyone the wrong props, the band was off key, and Jake couldn't get any sound to come out of his trumpet.

The skits were even worse. Everyone forgot their lines or missed their cues.

My group rehearsed our skit twice. The second time, Zan slipped and hurt her ankle. She acted like someone had cut her foot off with a buzz saw.

"My foot, my foot," she moaned.

Mrs. Kampton ran over and knelt down next to Zan. "It doesn't appear to be broken," she said, carefully touching the ankle. "You should go to the nurse's office, though. Can you walk?"

Zan limped around. "A little."

"I can help her," Pete offered. He walked out with his arm around Zan's shoulders. She leaned against him and looked much too happy for a person who was supposed to be suffering.

After she left, Mrs. Kampton helped us hang the backdrop that Beth had painted. It was really neat. The whole thing was big interconnecting circles. In the center of the circles were designs. There was something for every act: a big trumpet, an umbrella and some rain, and flames shooting up into the sky.

Mrs. Kampton had to go upstairs to check on the spotlight. Right after she left, Zan came back. She was wearing an Ace bandage and was hanging onto Pete's shoulder.

We all gathered around to look at her bandage. "Pete was so wonderful," Zan purred. "He even held my hand in the nurse's office." Pete looked down, embarrassed.

I was so angry I could feel my ears getting red. That is not the way your boyfriend is supposed to behave. Or your girlfriend either. I was just about to say something, when Zan saw the backdrop.

"What is this, this thing?" Zan shrieked, pointing to the set.

"It's the set," Beth answered firmly. "Don't you like it?"

"I hate it, and you knew I would," Zan yelled. "We talked about the backdrop. You agreed that you'd do it based on the magazine pictures I gave you."

"Yes," Beth said, "and I did." She walked over to the multicolored circles. "Here's the picture of the building on fire you gave me. See," she said, pointing, "in the middle is the fire. See the flames shooting out?"

Zan put her hands on her hips and glared at Beth. "What I see is that you're a liar," Zan said in her nastiest voice.

"Everything you gave me is here. I just made it a little more interesting, that's all."

"You ruined it," Zan moaned.

Suddenly I spoke up. "I like it."

"Who asked you?" Zan screamed. "Are you the director?"

"The show was my idea," I said, "and I like it."

"Well , I don't," Zan said. "So there."

"It's too late to change it anyway," Beth said. "The show is tomorrow."

"I hate you," Zan said. "You try to ruin everything." She turned and marched backstage.

"Wow," I said.

"That backdrop must have cured your ankle," Beth yelled to Zan, "because you seem to be walking fine on it now." As soon as Beth spoke , Zan went back to limping.

Phony, I thought.

"I have to sit down," announced Delia. "That was too much for me." She flopped down on the floor.

"Yeah, me, too." Beth sat next to her. I dropped down on the floor beside them.

"It was nice of you to stand up for me," Beth said. "I'm sorry I didn't talk to you for so long."

"Me, too," I said. "I really missed you." Beth and I smiled at each other. I was glad we were friends again.

After rehearsal I didn't feel like seeing anyone. I walked home slowly, thinking about how mean Zan was acting. She knew Pete was my boyfriend, yet she tried to get him away from me. The fact that we were friends didn't seem to mean anything to her. Annie would never do anything like that, and I bet Beth wouldn't either, I thought.

Then I started thinking about myself. I hadn't been very nice lately, not to Beth or Delia or Mary or Flora. Tomorrow, I'll make it up to them, I promised myself.

I was strolling through town thinking about this when Beth and Delia ran into me. "We're going to the Sweet Shop. Want to come?" Beth asked.

"Sure. Why not?" I replied.

We walked over to the Sweet Shop and grabbed a booth in the back. For almost an hour we sat around talking and giggling. We talked about everything: the show, Zan's behavior, Pete, our schoolwork.

I'm having fun, I thought. For the first time since Annie left, I'm really having a good time.

Chapter 10

When I got to the auditorium for the sixth–grade assembly the next evening, I was so nervous I could feel my legs shaking. I couldn't talk to anyone, not even to Annie, who had arrived at my house about an hour earlier.

I left Annie with Andrew and my folks and ran backstage to join the rest of my class. Mrs. Kampton was already there, helping everyone with their costumes and makeup. We were just about to go on, when the janitor came in with a message: The lighting man hadn't shown up.

"All right, class," Mrs. Kampton said. "I'm going to have to go up to the balcony and run the spotlight. We've rehearsed the show many times. I know you all know what to do," she said, laying a hand on Delia's head. "Make me proud now." Mrs. Kampton smiled at us, then left.

I could feel a knot tightening in my stomach. I looked around and could see that everyone else was nervous also. Delia was so white, she looked like a ghost.

A few minutes later the house lights went off. Delia pulled the curtain open, and Clarence, our Master of Ceremonies, stepped out.

The first act was Jake and his band. They were pretty good. Only one thing went wrong. Delia forgot to set up the triangle. So at the end of the number, Nathaniel, who was supposed to ring it, had to sing "ding." It was pretty funny, actually, and the audience laughed.

The tap dancers came next. I'd never realized what a good dancer Mary was. Edith and Flora just did some easy steps behind her, but Mary was really good. She got a big hand from the audience.

"That was really great, Mary," I said when she came backstage.

"Thanks," she replied curtly, not even looking at me. I felt bad. I knew I hadn't been very nice to her lately.

Our skit was last. When we got onstage, my heart was beating so fast that I didn't think I'd be able to say my lines. But once the skit started, I relaxed. My part was at the end. I was supposed to yell, "Liar, liar, pants on fire," then throw a bucket of confetti on Zan.

I threw my bucket. I could hear the whole audience sucking in their breath. Something was wrong. I looked at Zan. She was covered in green paint, and boy was she mad!

The audience began clapping and yelling. Zan went on bravely, pretending to shrink like she was supposed to. I was glad I didn't have any more lines, because I wasn't sure I could speak. A minute later the skit ended.

In a daze, I took my bows with the rest of the class. I'll never forget the sight of Zan smiling and bowing while green paint dripped from her dress onto her new shoes.

After the curtain came down, Zan turned to me and started to scream. "You idiot!" she yelled.

"Zan, I'm so sorry," I moaned.

"You're not sorry," she screamed. "You did it on purpose!"

"I didn't. I swear," I said, nearly in tears.

"Kathy wouldn't do that," Pete said.

"Yes, she would." Zan was doing this phony sobbing thing into her handkerchief. She had green paint all over her face. I hoped it would never come off.

"No one could have an accident like that," Rochelle said. "I bet she did it because she's jealous of all the attention you've been paying to Zan," she said to Pete. Everyone looked at Pete. He opened his mouth to speak, then closed it again.

"I know she did it on purpose," Zan said. "I saw her messing around with those buckets before the show started." All the kids glared at me.

"I never touched those buckets. You're lying," I said, outraged. I looked at the other kids, and I could tell no one believed me.

"Yeah, sure," Mary said, making a face at me.

90

"Come on, Mary," I said. "You know I wouldn't do that."

"Don't give me that 'come on Mary' stuff," she said to me. "You haven't been very nice lately and you know it."

"Yeah," Flora said. "Everyone knows how mean you've gotten since you started hanging out with Zan."

I looked at their angry faces. Didn't anyone believe me?

"I did not throw the paint on Zan on purpose," I yelled, "and that's final." I marched into the dressing room and burst into tears. Delia and Beth were waiting for me.

"You've got to tell her, Delia," Beth said. Delia just stood there with her head down. "Delia has something to tell you," Beth said.

Delia looked at the floor. "I accidentally gave you the wrong bucket," she whispered. "The whole thing was my fault. I'm sorry." Delia buried her head on Beth's shoulder and began to cry.

"You're sorry!" I yelled.

"That's right," Beth said. "She's sorry. She didn't do it on purpose, any more than you poured paint on Zan on purpose. And she's going to go out and tell everyone right now." Beth grabbed Delia's arm and pulled her outside.

I washed my face, then followed a minute or so later. Zan was talking.

" 'I'm sorry' isn't good enough," she was saying to Delia. "You'll have to pay for my dress, too."

Delia hung her head. "I'll try." I knew Delia would never be able to afford to pay for Zan's clothes.

"You know she won't be able to do that," I said.

"That's her problem, isn't it?" said Zan, nastily. She put her hands on her hips and glared at me.

"Well, it was my fault, too," I said. I handed Zan a five-dollar bill. "Here."

"Five dollars," Zan said scornfully. "That won't even pay for the socks."

"Here," Beth said, reaching into her bag. "I have three dollars."

"And I have seven," Pete said. He took some money out of his pants' pocket and handed it to Zan. Then everyone was digging into their pockets. Soon Zan's hands were full of money, and boy was she embarrassed.

"There, that should do it," I said.

"Thank you all," said Delia. She looked like she might start crying again.

"Get something in blue," I told Zan. "Green isn't really your color." Zan stomped off to change, followed by Rochelle and Lauren.

I looked after them. "Think they'll ever speak to me again?" I asked Beth.

"It will probably blow over in a few days," Beth said.

"Yeah," I said. "Is that why you didn't speak to me for so long?"

"I'm the kind of person who holds a grudge," Beth said, looking a little embarrassed.

I looked at Beth and Delia. "Are we all friends now?" I asked.

"Yeah," said Beth. We smiled at each other.

Pete came over to me. I gave him my best smile. "Do you want to come to the Sweet Shop with me and some of the other kids?" he asked.

"None of us has any money," I said. "And Annie is here. Why don't we all go over to my house for some ice cream?"

"Sounds good," Pete said.

I turned to Beth and Delia. "You want to come?"

"Sure," they said.

I walked into the dressing room. Rochelle and Lauren were trying to scrub Zan's dress. Zan had gotten most of the paint off her face, but her hair was still a mess.

"Hi," I said to them.

No one answered. "A bunch of kids are coming over to my house for ice cream. Would you like to come, too?"

Zan looked at me, her steely blue eyes as cold as ice. "Can't make it," she said. Lauren and Rochelle just shook their heads no.

"Some other time then," I said. But I knew that some other time wouldn't be any time soon.

When I got outside, Beth and Annie had already become friends. I walked in between them, with Pete and his group of friends behind us.

So I wasn't in the In Crowd any more. I had my own crowd. They might not be the coolest kids in the world, but I liked them. I turned to Pete. I took his arm and together we led the crowd back to my house.